What can you Stack on the Back of a Yak?

By Alison Green

Illustrated by Adam Stower

This is a yak, and a duck -
   Captain Quack.
They deliver the post
   to the mountains and back.
Each day Captain Quack
   leads them straight up the track
With the parcels piled high
   on the back of the yak.

"Four boxes, three sacks and two packets!" sings Yak.

"And, sitting on top of them, one Captain Quack!"

"Boxes and mail sacks and packets," sings Quack.

"Carefully, carefully, straight up the track."

But Yak's a bit naughty.
Yak likes to play.

He scoots off the track
and goes leaping away!

"Look, Captain Quack!
I can hop! I can prance!
Do you think, if they try,
yaks can learn how to dance?"
"No!" shouts the duck.

"Look out for those rocks!

"Yak, what have you done? You've smashed every last box!"
"Oops!" says the yak, and he sheds a big tear.

Then a voice from above calls ...

"We're stuck! Look up here!"

"Four baa-lambs!" says Yak.
"And they're trapped, Captain Quack!
Don't panic!" he shouts.
"You can jump on my back!"

"Four baa-lambs, three sacks and two packets," sings Yak.
"And, sitting on top of them, one Captain Quack."
"Mail sacks and packets and - baa-lambs?" huffs Quack.
"In my day we just carried post up the track."

But Yak's got the fidgets.
He longs to be free.

"Do you think, if they try,
yaks can climb up a tree?"

"No!" shouts the duck. "Please, keep to the track! Yak, what have you done? You've lost every last sack!"

"Oops!" says the yak, and he sheds a big tear.

Then a scratchety voice calls . . .

"We're lost! Over here!"

"Three chickens?" cries Yak.
"And they're all in a flap!
Hop on and hold tight.
Captain Quack's got a map!"

"Four baa-lambs, three chickens,
two packets," sings Yak.
"And, sitting on top of them,
one Captain Quack!"

"Packets - and baa-lambs!
  - and **chickens!**" scowls Quack.
"Behave yourself, Yak,
    and walk straight up the track!"

But Yak's playing cowboys.
"Quick! Fire at that shack!
The baddies are hiding there -
Cover my back!"

"What baddies?" shouts Quack.
"Now, stop all that racket.

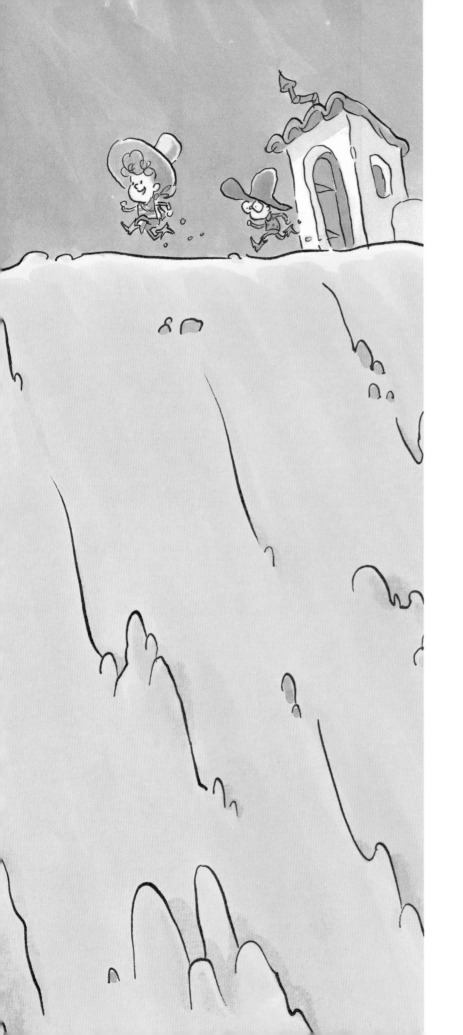

"Yak, what have you done?
  You've lost every last packet!"
"Oops!" says the yak,
  and he sheds a big tear.

Then the shed door flies open -
two cowboys appear!
"Howdy!" they cry.
  "My name's Zak!" "And I'm Jack.
We're late for our tea -
  can we ride on your back?"

"Four baa-lambs, three chickens,
two cowboys," sings Yak.
"And hanging on grumpily,
one Captain Quack!"

"Cowboys! And baa-lambs!
And chickens!" sighs Quack.
"What will the Mayor say,
when we get up the track?"

But Yak hasn't finished – he's found five tired hogs . . .

Six hitch-hiking rabbits . . .

and seven hot dogs . . .

Eight sleepy kittens
. . . and nine sleepy cats . . .
And, steering well clear of them,
ten ratty rats!

"Ten rats and nine cats and eight kittens," sings Yak.

"Seven dogs and six rabbits, all stacked on my back.

Five hogs and four lambs and three chickens," sings Yak.

"Two very small cowboys and . . . one Captain Quack!"

"Hold steady!" cries Quack, "and cling on to Yak's back!
If we're careful, we'll still make it straight up the track."

When they get to the village,
Quack says, "Hold it there!
I'd better go first
and explain to the Mayor . . ."

"No letters?" the Mayor cries. "No boxes? Alack!
You're fired, Captain Quack! Both you and your yak!"

"I'm sorry," says Quack, and he sheds a big tear.
Then a voice from outside calls . . .

"Hey!
Look who's out here!"

"My pet rats!" a girl cries.
"I thought you were lost!"
"My cats and my kittens!"
exclaims Mrs Frost.

"My dogs!" roars Old Henry.
"What wonder! What joys!"

"Our six long-lost rabbits!"
shout two little boys.

"My hogs and my baa-lambs!"
yells Farmer McTell.

"My three missing chickens!"
calls shopkeeper Nell.

And as for the Mayor, he's as pleased as can be:
"My two little cowboys! You're late for your tea!
Yes, it's tea-time for everyone! Please, I insist!
We'll lay on a spread that you just can't resist!"

"Three cheers!" cries the Mayor,
"For Quack and his yak!
For carrying everyone
safe up the track!"

For Harry, Ben and Sam
~ love from Alison

For Eirene and Rob, with love
~ from Adam

First published in 2013 by Alison Green Books
An imprint of Scholastic Children's Books
Euston House, 24 Eversholt Street
London NW1 1DB
A division of Scholastic Ltd
www.scholastic.co.uk
London – New York – Toronto – Sydney – Auckland
Mexico City – New Delhi – Hong Kong

This edition published exclusively for Scholastic Book Clubs and Fairs.

ISBN: 978 1 407139 00 5

1 3 5 7 9 8 6 4 2